THE
GOOD FORTUNES
GANG

ALSO BY MARGARET MAHY

Published by Delacorte Press

The Door in the Air and Other Stories

THE COUSINS QUARTET

THE GOOD FORTUNES GANG

MARGARET MAHY

ILLUSTRATED BY
MARIAN YOUNG

DELACORTE PRESS

Published by
Delacorte Press
Bantam Doubleday Dell Publishing Group, Inc.
1540 Broadway
New York, New York 10036

A Vanessa Hamilton Book

Library of Congress Cataloging in Publication Data

Mahy, Margaret.
    The good Fortunes gang / Margaret Mahy; illustrated by Marian
Young.
        p.   cm.
    Summary: After living like a gypsy in Australia all of his life,
Pete tries to adjust to living in a permanent place—his father's
New Zealand hometown where Pete must pass a test to belong to his
cousins' exclusive gang.
    ISBN 0-385-31015-3
    [1. Moving, Household—Fiction.   2. Cousins—Fiction.   3. New
Zealand—Fiction.]   I. Young, Marian, ill.   II. Title.
PZ7.M2773Go   1993
[Fic]—dc20   92-38784   CIP   AC

Manufactured in the United States of America

June 1993

10   9   8   7   6   5   4   3   2   1

Book design by Claire Vaccaro

TO MY WHAKATANE COUSINS—IN MEMORY OF HAPPY DAYS.

The Fortune Family Tree

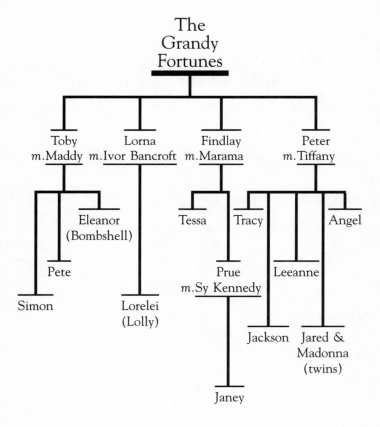

The
Grandy
Fortunes

Toby
*m.*Maddy

Lorna
*m.*Ivor Bancroft

Findlay
*m.*Marama

Peter
*m.*Tiffany

Eleanor
(Bombshell)

Tessa

Tracy

Angel

Pete

Prue
*m.*Sy Kennedy

Leeanne

Simon

Lorelei
(Lolly)

Jackson

Jared &
Madonna
(twins)

Janey

"Ice cream!" cried Pete's father, slowing the car as they drove into town. "I need instant ice cream." He glanced toward the back of the car, where Peter and his brother, Simon, sat on either side of Bombshell, the baby, in her car seat. They were snugly packed in with sleeping bags, windbreakers, pillows, and plastic bags of diapers. All the big stuff had gone on ahead of them in packing cases and was supposedly waiting for them in the new house.

"Shops!" cried Maddy, their mother, as if they had not seen shops for years. "I'm going to buy flowers." She opened the car door and scrambled out. "Then, when your mother actually sees me for the first time ever, I'll be carrying a big bunch of flowers for her. And I'll get some apples. Forget the ice cream! Ice cream's just junk food."

"Oh, come on, Mum," groaned Simon, impatiently flinging himself back among the sleeping bags. He was wearing black jeans and a black T-shirt and had spent his Christmas money having his hair dyed black. His eyebrows, however, were still fair . . . so fair that from some angles it looked as if he did not have any eyebrows at all. A thin gold earring shone in one ear. Simon looked like a teenage vampire with pimples. "We're healthy *enough*," he cried. "And there's a milk bar, right there!"

"That's not a milk bar," said his father, thrusting a red five-dollar bill at Pete. "It might be a milk bar in Australia, but we're in New Zealand now, and in New Zealand it's a dairy. Your mother can buy flowers at that shop down the road, but Pete will infiltrate the dairy and buy us ice cream. Your mother doesn't have to have one."

"I will have one, after all," said Maddy quickly, bending down to look through the window. "A vanilla cone. Not one of those lurid ones that looks as if it's all bruised and bleeding. And no chocolate chip! Nothing speckled. They make me think huge flies have been sitting on them."

"You certainly know how to take the fun out of ice cream," her husband grumbled. Pete climbed out of the car, holding the five-dollar bill tightly in case the wind tried to snatch it away from him. He slammed the door behind him. He was on his own in a new world.

Pete stood for a moment, glancing left and right. Although the shops looked ordinary enough, they were still shops in another country—a land of legend, for he was standing in Fairfield, his father's hometown. "I remember, back in Fairfield . . ." his father would say, beginning a hair-raising story of his own childhood. And now the shops were Fairfield shops, those hills beyond them were Fairfield hills, and the sky overhead was Fairfield sky. In a few minutes he would be meeting his New Zealand grandparents for the first time, and, that afternoon, relations from all over Fairfield would be gathering for a Fortune family reunion. The reunion, it was agreed, had to come before anything else. After that, Pete and his family would be free to begin unpacking and moving into their new house—which was also an old house, the very house his father had lived in when he was a boy.

The dairy, Pete found, turned out to be one of those shops that sells everything you might run out

of over the weekend and couldn't possibly do without. There was even a rack of videos for rent.

"*Zombie Vengeance: the dead arise and take re-
venge on the living*," the one nearest to him pro-
claimed in slimy green lettering.

"Four vanilla ice creams, please," Pete said to
the woman behind the counter and then looked
doubtfully at the five-dollar bill. It didn't look like
real money you could actually buy anything with.
Pete knew he would get used to it, though. A trav-
eler learned to get used to anything.

But then, as the woman reached for the ice
cream scoop, Pete heard a dreadful sound—half
whoop, half howl—coming from somewhere behind him. *Zombie vengeance*, he thought, and spun
around, clenching his fists and gritting his teeth,
prepared to go down fighting all the way. The wild
whoop became a fiendish shriek, rushing toward
the shop, growing louder and louder every moment. There was a whirr of wheels, and just as the
shriek dissolved into cackling wicked laughter, two
figures streamed past the shop—a boy and a girl,
both yelling and laughing as they shot by on skate-
boards. Pete saw the girl most distinctly. He stood
staring, even when there was nothing more to look
at, as chilly as if he had seen a ghost.

"Watch where you're going!" someone shouted angrily.

"I swear, those kids'll come to grief one of these days," said the woman behind the counter, patting generous scoops of ice cream into the cones.

But Pete was still staring at the space where the skateboarding girl had suddenly appeared and grinned at him. He had recognized her. Although he had been in town only ten minutes, he had recognized her: the girl from his worst nightmare.

Pete had been having this particular nightmare for as long as he could remember, but he had never gotten used to it. While he was dreaming, it was always as if it were happening for the first time, and it was always terrible. As he dreamed, every single thing he was fond of—everything that made home home—crept out of his room, while other unfamiliar things crept silently in and settled down as if they had always been there. Even the windows would slide around the walls, opening in different directions onto strange new views. His parents slid, too, tiptoeing around, picking up Bombshell and waking Simon. Finally all four of them would steal off through the front door, while two different parents and a strange, scowling big sister, with long fair hair and sharp blue eyes, tip-toed in through the back door. In his dream Pete would suddenly wake up and find himself sur-rounded by alien furniture and alien people. "Where are Mum and Dad?" he would ask the aliens. "Here we are, you silly boy," the aliens would say with terrible smiles. "We're your *real* parents and this is your sister. That other family, the ones you *think* you remember, were nothing but dreams."

The face that had flashed in and out of sight at the shop window—the face with the fierce smile and the wild, fair hair tossing around it—had been the face of the nightmare sister. Even though his hands were by now full of ice cream, Pete felt as if the wide-awake everyday world around him had actually become frail and thin, a curtain of cob-webs that he might accidentally brush away at any moment. He was here in Fairfield, the center of Fortune family stories. He was here, where, accord-ing to his father, they were going to stop traveling and settle down at last. But now it seemed that not only his father's family but Pete's own worst night-mare might be waiting for him here.

CHAPTER 2

It was later in the day when Pete next thought about his nightmare and the face he had glimpsed through the shop window. He stood in an upstairs room that was quite empty except for a bed and two suitcases. One was still unopened, but old jeans and a pair of underpants trailed out of the other, almost as if they were trying to escape and rush off to join in the Fortune family reunion without him. He was trying to imagine this room filled with his things—his books, his tapes, his posters— but it stayed obstinately empty.

"Pete!" called his mother from somewhere else in the house.

"Coming," he replied, but he did not move. Instead he looked out of the window across the tops of trees to the sea. The island on the horizon had a feather of smoke drifting from it. It was a volcano. Many years ago this room had been his father's room, and the sea and the volcano were what his father would have seen every single morning for years and years and years.

"Pete," called his mother again, "are you ready?"

"I said I was coming!" he called back.

He liked the straight, clear line where the sea met the sky. He liked the leaves that framed the view of the smoking island, and the rounded scoops of cloud behind it. All the same, as he had climbed out of the car and looked at the front of the house for the first time, Pete had had the second shock of the day. A second *sign*, he thought, that Fairfield was a more dangerous place than he had ever imagined it would be. He tried not to think about the tall hedge that he could see from his window, or the strange stone faces that had smiled at him through the leaves. No wonder Simon had given such a shout of triumph and had pointed and nudged him so sharply! But Grandma Fortune had pointed toward trees on the other side of the house.

"There's a path through the trees there to our

house," she had said. Pete was glad of an excuse to turn his back on the shadows, the hedge, and the stone faces.

"Pete!" his mother called for the third time. This time he knew she really meant it.

As he left his room, he turned left. But that was a direction that belonged to the last house he had lived in. "This is the day, but it isn't the way," he muttered to himself. Then he thumped downstairs, singing a Fortune family song that the house must have heard many times before:

"No matter how young a prune may be,
It's always full of wrinkles."

He wanted to let the house know he belonged in it.

Simon and Maddy were standing at the bottom of the stairs, face-to-face, like wrestlers searching for holds on one another.

"Spattzz!" muttered Simon, as Pete came downstairs. *Spattzz!* was a word Pete himself had invented so that he could swear when he needed to without being told off for it, but Simon had liked the sound of it. Already it was more his word than Pete's. "Spattzz and double spattzz! Just lis-

ten! He's going to be worse than ever, now we'll actually be living in Fortuneland for ever and ever."

"We'll see," said their mother.

"Do you mean we'll see if Pete gets worse, or we'll see if we're actually going to live here for ever and ever?"

"We'll see!" said Maddy, meaning, *Stop pestering me!*

"I know *you* don't want to live here," said Simon. "And Dad might change his mind in a week. I mean, he's made a few mistakes about places to live before now, hasn't he?"

"Don't you *want* to live in Fairfield?" Pete cried, staring at his mother. "I thought you did. You said you were sick of traveling with a baby."

"Who'd want to live a hundred miles from a proper city?" asked Simon. "And another thing . . . why have people been moving *out* of this house? The grandparents moved out three years ago, and Uncle Peter and his family moved in. Now Uncle Peter and his family have moved out, and *we're* moving in. There's something they're not telling us, and it's more than bad drains, because Uncle Findlay's a plumber, isn't he, so if it was drains, they could get them fixed cheaply."

"Grandma and Grandpa Fortune moved out because the house was too big for them," said Maddy.

"But it wasn't too big for Uncle Peter and his lot, though, was it?" Simon asked in a cunning voice. "I mean, they've got six kids!"

"Uncle Peter moved out because he bought a business with a house attached to it," their mother said, seizing Pete and looking him up and down as if she were planning to sell him and wanted him to look good.

"That's what they *say*," said Simon. "There's got to be more to it than that." He gave Pete a sly, considering glance. "I'll give you a clue. Think about what's over the hedge."

Before he could stop them, Pete's thoughts once more made a picture of the hedge and then sprang back from it as if it were red-hot.

"No matter how young a prune may be,
It has a worried look!"

he sang to himself. Simon let out a wailing cry.

"Why does he sing *those* songs?"

"Well, why have you dyed your hair black?

Why are you wearing an earring in one ear?" Maddy answered.

"That's different," Simon said impatiently. "That's modern . . . *trendy*. But nobody else in the world sings those double-spattzz, hairy old songs . . . nobody except Dad, and that thing there."

"Don't call your brother 'that thing there.' Pete looks all right. Now . . . what about you?"

"I look cool," said Simon.

"No matter how young a prune may be,
It's always getting stewed,"

sang Pete, rolling his eyes.

Simon's own eyes narrowed. He smiled in a sinister way that made his teeth look like fangs. "People leave this house because it's *haunted*," he hissed, while his mother peered into his face as if she were struggling to read something written in small print. But really she was just examining him for possible dirt.

"Let's be off!" cried Toby, Pete's father, bouncing through the doorway (Pete wasn't sure which room that door led to). His father was holding Bombshell, dressed up for the party his grandparents were preparing in the house on the other side of the trees.

It was all *Bombshell's* fault, Pete thought. If it hadn't been for her, Pete and his family might still be gypsies traveling around Australia, going from job to job, house to house, and school to school. But because Bombshell had forced her way into the family, here they were, standing among packing cases, preparing to meet the rest of the people belonging to all the family names found scrawled across Christmas cards or described in stories of long ago.

"Let's go!" said Pete's mother.

Toby led the way, carrying Bombshell, who waved her green bear over his shoulder. Pete and Simon fell in behind them. Simon nudged Pete. He was smiling his vampire smile again.

"Tonight you are going to have one of your ni-i-ightma-a-ares," he hissed in a low, mysterious voice, like a wizard pronouncing a spell.

> "Baby prunes look like their dad,
> But not wrinkled quite as bad,"

Pete sang defiantly.

"Don't forget," said Simon, "that from this day forward we're living next to a *graveyard*. Let's hear you sing about that!"

CHAPTER 3

"You'll love them all," cried Toby, jiggling Bombshell, who laughed and hit him over the head with her bear. "And they'll love you!" he added, hugging Pete's mother with his free arm.

"It's nice to see you so happy," Maddy said, smiling.

"Do I *have* to go?" Simon grumbled behind them. "I've already met the grandparents, and there's nobody else there . . . not anyone my age, I mean. All the cousins are just kids, like that thing there."

"Except for Prue," said his mother.

"But she's *married*," said Simon, as if being married was a terrible, catching sickness. "Well, she's *been* married. She's got a baby. She's old."

"Come on, Simon, don't be shy," said Toby.

"I'm not *shy*!" cried Simon angrily.

But suddenly Pete could see Simon might be shy, that he might be hiding his shyness behind a vampire smile. Pete didn't think he was shy himself. He was too used to starting at new schools halfway through the year and being stared at by everyone. Perhaps it was different for Simon.

Toby was the only wanderer of the Fortune family, yet his stories, told between packing and unpacking, were all about being in a single place with the same people. His stories were about his two brothers and his only sister, about tree houses, and dams across creeks, and a strange game of hide-and-seek called worraworra, played at night in the family forest—Fortune's Chase—that spread up the hill behind the house. Not only that, his songs were funny old songs he had learned from his own father, who had learned them from *his* father. By now, Pete could sing them all, too—"Nellie the Nudist Queen," "I Scream, You Scream, We All Scream for Ice Cream," and "The Prune Song." No matter what else changed, the songs stayed the same—always friendly, always jolly.

Pete's family walked across the veranda, down

the steps, and onto the lawn. Ahead of them the hill dropped away, and they could look out over the open sea. Shadows nibbled at the golden light washing the lawn, giving it a jigsaw-puzzle edge. Pete turned his face toward the sunshine, but Simon nudged him and glanced meaningfully at the tall, dark hedge in the shadow behind them.

Pete laughed and looked back casually. There, staring through the leaves at the very top of the hedge, he saw once more those three faces . . . gray faces patched with moss, watching him and smiling with closed, secret lips.

"Heh! Heh! Heh!" said Simon, giving a soft, vampirish chuckle.

Somehow Pete's father had never mentioned the old graveyard in any of his stories, let alone the tall hedge that hid most of it. Three gray angels, though, were taller still, and they peered over the top of the hedge like nosy neighbors watching someone else's family life.

Simon nudged Pete again.

"Spooky! Spooky! Spooky!" he said.

"I'm not frightened of ghosts," Pete muttered. Yet losing a family, even in a dream, was like a sort of death. And having that same nightmare over and over again was almost like being haunted. Living next to a graveyard would only give the nightmare power.

Passing through a little rickety gate, Pete and his family followed a track that wound through the bush (they called forests "bush" in New Zealand, just as they did in Australia). Trees rose up around them, closing them in with leaves and shadows. A net of thin, twisty, unknown paths branched off and vanished under fallen leaves. In the distance they could hear happy voices—sounds of Fortunes, meeting and already having a good time. Pete, remembering his father's stories of family picnics, imagined uncles and aunts bringing bowls of salad, chocolate cakes, and all sorts of other good things into Grandma Fortune's kitchen. And they would be bringing more than sausages and cakes. They would be bringing their children, too, of course.

Cousins! He was going to meet them and, in particular, four cousins his own age: Tessa (Uncle Findlay's daughter), Tracey and Jackson (Uncle Peter's kids), and Aunt Lorna's daughter, Lolly Bancroft, the only cousin who did not have Fortune for her last name. In a few minutes they would all become more than mere names. They would be round and real. For Pete, this reunion would be like the first day at a new school. In family stories Fortunes were always true to other Fortunes. In real life he might not like his cousins. And they might not like him.

The track under the trees of Fortune's Chase was soft with leaves and fringed with ferns. Pete and his family walked over speckles of gold. The trees tangled green fingers over his head, and ferns swarmed up the banks on either side. Some ferns were as big as trees, with hairy trunks and leaves that were green above and silver below.

"On the track! No turning back!" Pete whispered to himself, talking in rhyme as he often did when he talked to himself. In spite of everything, he didn't want to turn back, but when he suddenly saw steps cut into the bank, he couldn't help stopping and staring, trying to work out where they led to. Looking into the branches above, he saw a great black patch like the nest of a dragon, nestled among the leaves of a big tree. There seemed to be some sort of climbing rope dangling from it. But as he stared upward, Bombshell threw her green bear at him, hitting him on the ear.

"Pick that up, will you?" asked his father. Pete picked up the toy and followed his family once more—out through the leaves and into a bare gar-

den filled with lots of people, who all turned and stared at them. Shouts of welcome sounded like one shout. Smiles seemed like one smile. But there was no smile on the only face Pete could see that was more or less on a level with his. A thin girl with fair, straggly hair and bright blue eyes was actually scowling at him. Then uncles and aunts pressed forward, beaming and holding out their hands and arms, and the girl was hidden.

Pete suddenly saw himself as she must have seen him, coming out of the bush holding a green bear, just as if he were a little kid who needed a toy to comfort him. But that was not the worst thing. The worst thing was that the fair, straggly hair and bright blue eyes belonged to his nightmare sister. She had been waiting for him, already more a part of the family than he was.

CHAPTER
4

Suddenly there were Fortunes all around him, telling him their names. So this was Uncle Findlay, fair and freckled, and this was Aunt Marama, with black hair piled on top of her head and dark Polynesian skin. "Pete, here's Uncle Peter, the one you were named after," said his mother. "And this is Aunt Tiffany." Pete knew it would take him a long time to remember which face belonged to which aunt or uncle. He just smiled, let the uncles shake his hand and pat his back, and let the aunts kiss him. They didn't really want him to say much, just to smile and show he was happy to be among them. As for the cousins, there were cousins everywhere.

The tallest and oldest was Prue, who was Uncle

Findlay's daughter, and she was holding a baby older than Bombshell. They were still living with Uncle Findlay and Aunt Marama, although she was nineteen and had once been married. For the family reunion, Prue had chosen to wear an old, white dress of floating material that had been painted with golden suns and silver moons. She also wore black lace tights, and sneakers dyed green. Pete noticed Simon's mouth fall open for a moment when he first saw Prue. Then he saw him grin, thrilled to have a cousin who looked almost as trendy as he thought he did himself.

Meanwhile, Leeanne, the middle daughter of Uncle Peter and Aunt Tiffany, stared at Simon, and then began to follow him. She was about eight years old and carried a Barbie doll. Simon pretended not to see her.

Most of the other cousins were small. Several of them were babies whose names Pete could not remember, and there were Uncle Peter's three-year-old twins. People smiled at the babies, trying to make them smile back, and told one another over and over again that the babies were "real Fortunes." If they stayed here . . . if they *did* stay . . . Bombshell would grow up with cousins of her own age all around her.

"Peter, this is Lorelei," said yet another aunt
. . . his father's sister, Lorna Bancroft. Pete
turned, half expecting to see the scowling girl. But
this was an entirely different cousin. Lorelei Bancroft was smiling a timid, apologetic smile. Though
she was ten and almost as old as Pete, she looked
so shy that Pete immediately felt shy too. When
she smiled, she covered her mouth with her hand
so that people couldn't see her wired-up teeth.
They looked at each other in silence.

"Everyone calls me Pete, not Peter," Pete said
at last.

Lorelei uncovered her mouth. "Everyone calls
me Lolly," she replied. "Even my mother does,
when she's not thinking. Did you get that Christmas card I sent you?"

Pete suddenly remembered Lolly's Christmas
card. It had had a picture of Santa Claus filling the
Christmas stocking of a dinosaur, and she had
drawn it herself. "It was great," he said politely.

"The dinosaur was a diplodocus," said Lolly.
"They'd have had enormous stockings! Are you
glad to be here?"

"It's okay," said Pete. "Okay so far!"

"Lolly," said a voice. It was her father, Pete's

uncle Ivor. "Your mother says she's left the keys in the car. Would you run down and get them for me?"

Lolly set off. She did not invite Pete to go with her, and, left on his own again, he moved through the crowd, grinning and nodding. Where were the other cousins who were his age? Were they actually hiding from him? He wondered how it was that he could feel that he didn't want to meet them and yet at the same time feel that he had been wanting to meet them ever since he was a baby.

"How do you think *you'll* like living here, though?" asked a voice somewhere over his head. It was Prue talking to his mother.

"Well, it's fine so far," said his mother, "and this is a great party."

To Pete's surprise Prue laughed.

"You don't have to be polite about it—not to me," she said. "Did you really *want* to settle down here? After living in Brisbane and Rockhampton and Mackay and all those other places?"

Maddy laughed too. When she spoke, her voice sounded happier for some reason.

"I don't know," she said. "We certainly mean

to try, but by now it's hard to imagine really set-
tling down, in spite of all the talk. Toby's always
been restless. And Fairfield is a small town."

Big enough to hold the Fortune family,
thought Pete. Big enough to hold his father's stories of family worraworras. He remembered his old
blue jeans and underpants trying to escape from
his suitcase. Suppose they simply wanted to get out
of the suitcase and settle down? But in his imagi-
nation the suitcase sucked them back into itself,
tidied itself up, closed its own lid, and locked itself.
It was like a film running backward. Pete suddenly
realized that after such a lengthy journey and all
the stories, he wanted to stay in Fairfield for a
long, long time. But was there any point in trying
to find cousins who didn't want to be found? Was
there any point in making them notice you when
your father might get restless, in spite of all his
promises?

A few steps farther on he came across his father
talking to Uncle Peter. Pete listened. To his surprise they were talking as stiffly and politely as he
and Lolly had been talking a moment earlier. They
did not sound like brothers who had built dams
together and played worraworra in the bush at

night. If one of them made a joke, the other one sounded unsure about just when to laugh.

"How do you think you'll enjoy being back here?" Uncle Peter was saying. Everyone was asking the same question.

"Well, it's *home*," Toby said, sounding slightly indignant.

"Home? What do you mean by home, these days? Let's face it, Toby, you've been away for years," Uncle Peter replied. "You must have changed."

"Hi," said a voice so close to Pete's ear that he knew before he turned that someone his size was speaking to him. "Me again!" While Pete had been working his way in a rough circle around his grandparents' garden, Lolly had found the car keys and given them to her father.

By now Pete had a question to ask her. "Aren't the other cousins here?"

"Yes, but they sneaked off," said Lolly. "I saw them going into the bush. They're probably having a gang meeting."

"A gang?" It sounded like good fun. "Why didn't you sneak off too?" Pete asked.

"They call it the Good Fortunes Gang, and my

name's Bancroft, not Fortune," Lolly said. "Only people called Fortune can belong to it."

This seemed unfair to Pete. It wasn't Lolly's fault that Aunt Lorna had had to change her name to Bancroft when she married. He looked at Lolly, trying hard to work out if she felt sad at not belonging to the Good Fortunes Gang.

"What do they do?" he asked.

She shrugged. "I don't know," she said. "I only hear them talking about it. Tessa wants to call it the Fortune Investment Society and make money. But Tracey and Jackson want it to be a gang of radical revolutionaries hiding out in the forest."

"My name's Fortune," said Pete. "I could belong." And suddenly he made up his mind that he would find the gang and show them that *he* was a Fortune and that they could not keep him out simply by scowling and hiding. The steps! he thought. The steps cut into the bank! The dragon's nest up in the tree!

"Shall we track them?" he asked. "Shall we find them and make them let us join the club?"

"It's hard to make Tracey do anything if she doesn't want to," said Lolly doubtfully. All the same, she seemed to be considering his idea. But at that moment her father called her again, and once more Pete was left on his own.

He looked around. Uncles and aunts were everywhere, talking or fussing over little kids. Simon was talking to Prue. His parents had their backs to him. No one noticed him setting out all alone into the forest, searching for people he had never met before, who obviously did not want to meet him.

CHAPTER 5

These trees were all Fortune trees, the path that led between them was a Fortune path. Pete was a Fortune, and he had come home. All the same, this forest he was walking through did not feel like his forest—not yet. It was watching him, not welcoming him.

Pete walked on between trees and ferns that would always be green, for this was a land where the only trees that lost their leaves in autumn came from other countries. He imagined himself as a tree growing among these Fortune trees, as green and leafy as any other tree. Suddenly winter would come. All his leaves would drop off, leaving him naked to the icy wind. Everyone would see at a glance that he didn't belong in that particular forest.

Behind him he could hear the babble of the family reunion, but as he rounded a bend, he suddenly heard new voices. They were faint but clear and seemed to be coming out of the air. Pete moved softly, careful not to snap twigs or rustle ferns. The voices were talking about money.

"We've got five dollars and sixty-three cents," one voice was saying. "My vote is that we save it up and buy shares with it. You know—invest it! We could be rich by the time we're twenty."

"Twenty! No way! Too long, man! I won't *live* to be *twenty*," said a second voice, sounding very cheerful.

"Well, *I* vote we slide down to the road by one of the tracks and invest the money in fish and chips right now," said a third voice. "I'm not going back to be reunioned with Australians."

"They're half New Zealanders," said the first voice.

The voices, Pete realized, were up in the dragon's nest . . . the biggest nest in the world. No. Not a nest. A platform! Pete had found a Fortune family tree house, and the Good Fortunes Gang was having a meeting. What now? Should he shake the tree and force his cousins to notice him? He imagined shaking it with super strength so that cousins came tumbling down like ripe apples.

"It's not a crime, and now's the time," he muttered, and began pulling his way up steps in the bank, grabbing handfuls of ferns, and then a nobbly root, to steady himself.

"I've really *had* it with family reunions. Who cares!" said the third voice. "I'm not going to be friendly with kids who pushed us out of our house."

"Your dad bought the car yard," the first voice said. "You'd have moved anyway."

Peter knew at once that the nobbly root was used to being held. Other hands had polished it. The narrow steps fitted his size of foot exactly. A tug, a heave, and he was safely up, one hand on the tree trunk. A rope with knots in it—a climbing rope—dangled from the branch, and there were slats of wood nailed to the side of the tree, making a rough ladder. Pete thought the rope would be the most daring way to climb. He kicked off his sandals, seized the rope, and swarmed upward.

The people on the platform in the tree sud-

denly fell silent. They must have felt him struggling as he clambered, hand over hand, clamping
his feet around each knot, pushing upward, swinging like a monkey. No one looked out to help or
hinder him. Nailed to the edge of the platform was
a painted sign. THE GOOD FORTUNES GANG, it said in
faded, uneven lettering. As Pete read it, the rope
swung toward the sign until the words seemed as
big as the world. They were all he could see. A
moment later his nose was mashed against them.
Pete refused to groan. Instead he hooked the fingers first of one hand and then the other around
the edge of the platform and hung there, breathing
and letting his nose recover. Then he pulled himself up so that he was propped on his forearms,
looking over the edge of the platform.

Three faces stared back at him. That must be
Tessa, the younger sister of Prue, with black curls
and skin that was darker than her father's but paler
than her mother's. That must be Jackson, the boy
whose blond hair was clipped short and stubbly on
top, leaving long, pale locks hanging down around
his neck. Even though he was up a tree and in the
shade, Jackson had his nose covered with blue zinc
ointment. He looked like a surfer.

The third face was the one he already knew.

That was scowling Tracey, her hair as fair as Jackson's. Pete noticed how the other two looked at her as if she were their leader and they must follow her commands.

"Hi!" said Tessa at last, grinning widely. "Did Lolly tell you where we were?"

"Are you Pete?" asked Jackson. Then, without waiting for an answer, he asked, "What's it like in Australia?" He seemed to want to be friendly. But Pete saw Tracey push her knuckles firmly into his shoulder. Jackson fell silent, and the Good Fortunes Gang watched as Pete scrabbled and scrambled, uninvited, to swing a knee up onto the platform. None of them offered to help him.

CHAPTER
6

Now that he was on the tree-house platform, Pete felt he *must* make himself into a real Fortune. He must stop being a stranger swinging on a rope on the edge of things. But Pete could tell that Tracey was the one who did the inviting for all three cousins. And now, as he looked at her, he suddenly remembered a family photograph Uncle Peter and Aunt Tiffany had sent them years ago. Even as a little girl she had looked at the photographer with the same unsmiling and slightly menacing expression. That expression had somehow wormed its way into his dreams and had settled on the face of the false sister in his nightmare.

Jackson glanced sideways at Tracey and then

copied her suspicious expression as well as he could—though it didn't quite fit his kind of face.

"What are you doing here, man?" he asked, trying to make his croaky voice sound rough and stern. "This is *our* house."

"It says 'Good Fortunes,' " said Pete, pulling himself up and sitting on the edge of the platform. "And I'm a Fortune."

"Yes, but are you *good?*" Tessa asked, and he saw the beginning of a grin that would be wide and curly if she grinned properly.

"Pretty good," Pete said, grinning back.

Tracey spoke. She and Jackson both had croaky voices, but it was not because they had colds. It was just the way their voices always sounded.

"Tracey," she said, introducing herself, though Pete knew perfectly well who she must be. "Trace the Ace!" she added now, staring hard at Pete with her bright blue eyes. Pete knew she was eleven, a little older than he was. "Have you moved in yet?" she inquired as if she were asking a disagreeable question.

"We haven't unpacked," said Pete.

"Which room do *you* have?" she asked.

"It's upstairs," Pete said. "It's only a little one."

"Can you see the sea from the window?" she

asked, looking as thunderous as possible for someone who was so very fair. Pete nodded. "That used
to be *my* room," she cried, screwing up her eyes
angrily.

"My dad says it used to be his," Pete said
quickly. Tracey opened her eyes in astonishment.

"But that was ages ago," she said at last. "That
was in history. I'm talking about modern times."

Pete shrugged.

"It's not my fault," he said. "I just go where I'm
put."

"Anyhow, what are you doing up here?" asked
Jackson.

"Perhaps he wants to join our club?" suggested
Tessa, looking slyly at Tracey. "First, his name's
Fortune, and second, he could *pay* to join. We
need a new financial member." She looked over at
Pete and then rattled a tin cup at him.

"Hey, listen. He can't just waltz in here taking
over other people's bedrooms and calling himself a
Fortune," Tracey said, looking indignant from
one to the other.

"No way, man!" said Jackson, watching Tracey
and copying her.

"I didn't call myself a Fortune," Pete argued,
doing his best to stick up for himself and yet trying

to sound friendly at the same time. "I was born one."

"But you haven't lived here the way we have!" cried Tracey. Her white-blond hair seemed to shine in the dark. She did not look quite like a girl, but she did not look like a boy either. She looked like a burning creature from another world. "You've taken over the old house, *my* house, and everyone's making a fuss because your lot have come home at last. But that doesn't make you a real New Zealand Fortune—like we are."

The other two watched her respectfully. Pete hesitated, and Tracey saw him hesitate.

"Being a Fortune isn't just being *called* Fortune," she declared. "You get to be a true Fortune by going through the *Test*. The *Test* changes your blood."

She said the word *test* as if it were underlined. Somewhere in Pete's mind the word wrote itself in heavy black letters and sprouted scrolls of red and gold. Jackson and Tessa looked sharply at Tracey. Pete could see they did not have any idea of what she was talking about. She had invented the idea of the test only a minute before. All the same, Jackson leapt to his feet and began dancing on the spot, clapping his hands over his head and swaying from side to side. The platform trembled as he danced.

"Hey, man . . . the test, the test, the test!" Jackson cried. "You've got to do the test, man, and show you are the best, man, and then we'll be impressed, man! Yay, yay, yay," he sang. (Did rhymes run in the blood of the Fortune family? Pete wondered.)

Tracey thumped Jackson. Pete winced in sympathy. Jackson stopped dancing and fell silent, rubbing his leg where the thump had landed.

"I am secretary of this society," Tessa said in an important voice. She smiled to herself. "This must be recorded in the minutes," she went on, scribbling on a pad. "Will those in favor please say 'Aye'?"

"Yeah!" said Tracey.

Tessa turned to Tracey with an indignant look.

"You've got to say 'Aye,'" she insisted. "That makes it proper, legal society business. You don't just say 'yeah'—not for legal society business."

"Okay! Okay! Aye, then! Aye!" groaned Tracey.

"Ai, Ai, Ai!" cried Jackson, dancing again and pretending to play a guitar. Then he made a pecu-

liar rattling sound like drummers warming everyone up for "God Save the Queen."

"Jackson's musical," said Tessa, staring at Jackson proudly. "Are you musical?" she asked Pete.

"Everyone says I can't sing," said Pete, watching as Tracey wrapped one thin arm around Jackson's legs and yanked his feet from under him. When he crumpled down on top of her, she seized his ears and, using them as handles, wobbled his head from side to side. He didn't seem to mind.

"Say 'Aye' properly," she cried. "I had to."

"Aye!" cried Jackson, his voice more froggy than ever.

Tracey looked back at Pete.

"Can't you sing?" she asked him.

Pete actually thought he sang well, but no one in his family agreed with him. He thought he had better say no. Tracey looked pleased.

"But my dad plays the banjo," he added, to show there was music in the family. Tracey's blue eyes had seemed almost friendly. Now they grew sinister.

"Actually we can have the test straightaway," she said. "It's a word test. If you know the right words . . . well, that proves you're a good Fortune."

Pete's heart sank. How could he possibly know secret words when he'd only been in the country for one day?

Tracey nudged Jackson. "Okay! Sing a bit of that song and let him finish it," she commanded.

"What song?" asked Jackson.

Tracey nudged him again. "You know! That *prune* song!" she said.

CHAPTER 7

Jackson slowly stood up.

"This is a mystical Fortune song," Tracey announced. "Every Fortune who is a true Fortune knows the words of this song. Go on, Jackson."

Jackson looked as if he weren't too sure of the words himself. All the same, after a moment he began to sing.

"No matter how old a prune may be,
It's alway full of wrinkles . . ."

"Stop!" shouted Tracey. She looked at Pete challengingly.

"Finish that song!" she ordered. "Every true Fortune can finish that song."

Pete had known the song for so many years, the words were part of his memory. But just for the moment he couldn't think of one of them.

"Shall I sing it again?" Jackson asked.

"No! Once is enough," Tracey replied quickly.

But suddenly Pete remembered standing at the bottom of the stairs only half an hour ago, teasing Simon. Every single word of the song rushed back into his head, all jostling and anxious to be sung.

"It's 'young'!" he said. "Not 'old.' No matter how *young* a prune may be . . ." He began to sing.

"It's always full of wrinkles.
We may get them on our face.
Prunes get them every place."

He sang the first verse and chorus, then the second verse and chorus. The three cousins listened intently until Pete had finished the song.

"He got it right," said Tessa, sounding surprised.

"Yes, but that's just one song," said Tracey quickly. "Anyone can accidentally know *one* song. Jackson, do another."

"I scream, you scream, we all scream for ice cream," Jackson sang obediently. But after the first few words Pete joined in and sang too. When it came to the second verse, Jackson hesitated, pretending he was getting tired of singing, but Pete could easily see he had forgotten the words. Jackson might be able to sing in tune, but he didn't know things by heart, the way Pete did.

"What about 'Shut the Door, They're Coming Through the Window'?" suggested Tessa. She began to sing herself. Jackson and Pete joined in.

"Shut the door, they're coming through the
  window.
Shut the window, they're coming through the
  door.
Shut the door, they're coming through the
  window.
Oh, the place is full, and won't hold any more!"

Tracey did not sing along. Pete had said he couldn't sing, and she had been tricked into thinking that someone who couldn't sing wouldn't know the words. As Pete, Jackson, and Tessa sang the first verse and the chorus, and then the second verse and the chorus, Tracey looked more and more like the false sister of Pete's nightmare. Both Jackson and Tessa stopped singing at the end of the second chorus. They seemed to think the song was over. Pete hesitated.

"What about the third verse?" he asked.

"There isn't a third verse," said Tracey.

"Yes, there is," Pete cried. "I thought every single Fortune would know the third verse. If you don't know the *third* verse, you can't be a real Fortune."

Tracey looked sharply at Jackson. "Is there a third verse?" she asked.

Jackson shrugged so hard that his shoulders came right up to his ears.

"There is, and I know it, so that means I must be *more* of a Fortune than you because I know the songs better," cried Pete triumphantly.

Tracey's blue eyes seemed to drill through Pete.

"You can't possibly ever in this world be more of a Fortune than we are!" she cried.

"You said words were the test, and I know more words than you guys," Pete pointed out.

"Words are only *part* of the test," cried Tracey.

"Hey, Trace! Come off it," said Tessa. "Be fair!"

"Words are only the *first* part of the test," Tracey persisted. Anyone could tell she was thinking quickly, inventing a new test as she went along. "It's like taking a driver's test. You answer questions and then you do the *practical* part, the actual driving. He's still got to do the *practical* part."

"Shall I do it now?" asked Pete, full of confidence.

"Listen," said Tracey, "this reunion's probably going on for hours and hours. We've got sleeping bags and we'll be sleeping over at the old place—*our* old place, that is. It's a new place to *you*—while the grown-ups have their party. That's when we'll tell you what the *practical* test is. If you get through it, we'll count you as a real Fortune."

"Not fair!" began Tessa doubtfully. "We should vote. That's democratic."

"Jackson agrees with me," said Tracey. "That's democratic enough." Jackson wriggled his eyebrows up and down and swayed a little.

"Ai, ai, ai!" he sang softly.

"I'm not scared," Pete said. "I'll do any old test for fun. But I'm a real Fortune—no matter how it turns out."

Just for a moment he saw a flash of respect in Tracey's blue eyes. Just for a moment he saw the beginning of a smile.

"We'll see about that tonight," she said, looking tough once more. "All right, then! Let's go back to the great reunion barbecue. I'm hungry."

"The meeting of the Good Fortunes Gang is now adjourned," said Tessa, sounding grown-up and important. "Now we'll go to the grandies' for the barbecue and make out we're ordinary." She looked at Pete. "That's what we do," she said. "Pretend to be ordinary. But secretly we're radical, especially Jackson. He's radical *and* musical too."

"If anyone says anything bad about a Fortune, we get our gang on to them," Jackson said. "That's a gang rule. We even stick up for Lolly, though she's only a Bancroft and goes to the Catholic school. Come on . . . let's go!"

CHAPTER 8

Later that evening, well after the babies had been put to bed, Pete's mother, together with Aunt Lorna and Aunt Marama, led the older children along the track through Fortune's Chase to the old house.

Tracey nudged Pete.

"All *right!*" he whispered, before she could say anything. "I won't forget."

"It really *is* our house," said Tracey, "even if we don't live in it anymore. And now we're having to sleep out in the *whare*."

The *whare* was a little cabin with six bunks in the yard behind the old house. Pete hadn't even known it was there until the others told him about it. *Whare*, Tessa explained, was a Maori word meaning a home.

Lolly Bancroft was not allowed to sleep out in the *whare* . . . or perhaps she was too shy to ask. Her mother swept her into the big house, saying rather apologetically that Lolly was frightened of bush rats, but a little earlier Pete had heard Uncle Ivor complaining to Aunt Lorna that the *whare* was filled with rubbish. Separated from the other cousins, Lolly was tucked down in a spare bedroom at the foot of the stairs.

"And no tricks either," Pete heard Aunt Marama saying in a typically cynical mother's voice. Tricks? There were certainly going to be a few tricks after the grown-ups had gone back to the family reunion.

"Wait five minutes after your mother's gone and then come down and meet us in the yard," Tracey had said. "Say ten minutes, because sometimes our lot of wrinklies try to be clever and sneak back to check on Jackson and me."

"My mother trusts me," Tessa had smugly replied.

"What an idiot!" Tracey had muttered rudely.

In a way, Pete had enjoyed sitting on the sunny edge of his grandparents' lawn, eating sausages with his cousins while planning to sneak out at night. The idea of the test brought them together, though they were the testers and he was the one being tested. He tried not to think too much about what the test might be.

As he changed into his pajamas, Pete heard his mother talking to Lorna and Marama at the foot of the stairs. Then he heard Maddy climbing toward him. He dived into bed and tried to look sleepy.

"Well," she said, sitting on the edge of the bed. "How has it been so far?"

"Okay!" said Pete, pretending to yawn. Then he glanced over at her and found she was staring at him with a suspicious, motherly expression.

"Okay?" she said, and pretended to yawn too. "As good as that? Have the cousins been giving you a hard time?"

"No!" he exclaimed. "I'm not scared of them."

"Marama tells me that Tracey is a bit of a hard case."

"She's all right," said Pete. "I'm a hard case too."

His mother laughed and looked happier.

"I know you are," she said, and then gave him a kiss on his ear.

"Why do we have to go to bed now?" Pete asked.

"Because . . . !"

"Why because? Everyone else is having a good time."

"Because it's late, and, party or no party, we've got a busy day tomorrow. Unpacking! Mind you, I don't think your father will feel like getting up early."

She turned to go, pausing at the doorway to switch out the light.

"Mum . . ." Pete called softly after her.

"Yes?"

He could not see her face, just her black shape in the doorway.

"Mum, have the aunts been giving *you* a hard time?"

"No," she said. "If anything, just the opposite. They've been a bit too nice to me. It makes me feel like a visitor."

"Mum, don't you want to live here forever?"

"Nothing lives anywhere forever," she answered.

"No, but you know what I mean."

Pete was quite prepared for her to say, "We'll

see!" but she didn't. Instead she seemed to think about it, a faceless black shape leaning in the doorway.

"Well, do *you*?" she said at last.

Pete had to think about this.

"I sort of do," he said at last. "I want to have a place that stays still."

"Places stay still. We're the ones that keep moving," she replied. "And if we don't move one way, we move another."

"Tracey and Jackson say we took their house," he said.

"Well, we didn't," his mother replied. "Uncle Peter just decided to move out months before we decided to move in. Uncle Peter gave up the crane-hire business, and your father's taken it on. We'll give it a go, shall we? I know it's all strange, but we're used to that. So let's be patient and see what happens."

"I won't enjoy it if you don't," he said.

His mother sighed.

"Well, my family isn't as big as your father's," she said at last, "and I don't think I'll miss them in the way your father missed his family. Oh, he wanted to get away from home all right, but once he was away from it, nowhere else ever felt like the right place to him. But as for me . . . I don't know how happy I'm going to be staying here. How can I tell until I've tried?"

"Will I have to cheer for the New Zealand cricket team now?" asked Pete.

"No way," said his mother. "You cheer for whomever you want to, mate. Now, go to sleep. And if you dream, wake up and turn the flashlight on. It's right beside your bed."

"I'm not scared of dreams . . . well, just that *worst* dream," said Pete. "The dream of the false family."

"Well, I've noticed that whenever we move, that dream comes back," said his mother. "Just laugh at the false family. *We're* the real one."

"In the dream they say they're real, and it *seems* real," Pete groaned.

"Laugh at them," she repeated. "Shine the light on them."

"Mum," said Pete. "Tracey looks like the girl in my dream."

"Really?" said his mother. She sounded interested. "It'll be because of that photograph of her. Remember, we used to have all those family photographs pinned to the wall when we were living in Mackay. There was a photograph of Tracey. She was only little then, of course, but she still looked a really hard case. I think she was probably even a hard-case baby. If you'd like me to stay close for a while, I will."

Pete was tempted. He could imagine himself saying, "I would have joined you and gone through the test, no trouble at all, but my mother was feeling lonely. I had to keep her company." But the cousins would probably guess the truth. And besides, he wanted them to admit what he himself already knew: that he was just as much a Fortune as they were.

"I'm fine," he said. He pulled the blankets around his ears. His mother smiled, turned out the light, and went downstairs.

CHAPTER 9

When it felt as if his mother must be safely back with the other grown-ups, Pete got up again, put on his bathrobe, seized the flashlight, and went boldly downstairs. His light picked out packing cases and boxes. *This isn't* anyone's *home,* thought Pete. *Not anymore. Not yet!* But if he passed the test, he would win a home as his reward. He went out into the backyard.

It was a moony night. Could that possibly be the same moon Pete had seen in Australia a day or two earlier, a bright, thin sideways smile in the early evening? Now it was rounder and whiter, and seen from a different country. Pete looked up at it, imagining it was an opening of some kind and that

aliens, hidden on the other side of the sky, were sucking colors out of the world. *"Mmmm! Red!"* he imagined them saying. *"Blue . . . delicious!"*

Pete shone the light around. The backyard certainly looked colorless and completely empty. He hoped his cousins had all gone to sleep. Then he would be able to go back to bed. "Some test!" he would say in the morning, smiling scornfully. "Walking all the way downstairs and then back up again. Really hard! Really scary." But then a shadow on the edge of the other shadows waved at him. He sighed and made his way across the yard.

"You won't need a flashlight," Tracey said as Pete came up to them.

"You know your way around and I don't," he answered quickly, switching the flashlight on and swinging the beam of light around the yard. Tracey was holding a pillow. Behind her, Jackson seemed to be carrying the skin of a giant caterpillar over his shoulder.

"Let him have it," said Tessa. "Let's record the beginning of the test." She lifted her arm and stared at her own wrist as if she were checking some delicate instrument strapped there. "Test begun at twenty-one hours." However, she could not possibly have read her watch in the silver-gray light of the moon.

"Tessa's got a watch that still goes when you're a thousand fathoms under the sea," Tracey told Pete. "It tells you the time in Tokyo, and it tells you whether it's going to be a new moon or not." She was leading the way out of the yard and around the side of the house. She moved quickly, even in the dark. It was as if she remembered paths the way Pete remembered the words of songs.

But then, suddenly, Pete knew exactly where they were taking him. The night was warm, but he turned cold with horror. Every part of him longed to scramble back into bed and sink into immediate sleep. He did not want to be out in the night following his cousins toward the graveyard.

The high, uneven hedge of laurels blocked their way. Pete could not see any angels or ghosts, but he could feel their blank eyes peering around for him. Suddenly he felt that those angels had always been there in his nightmare, staring in at the sliding windows of the changing house, smiling at his confusion and horror.

"Through here," whispered Tracey. "Lucky we're not too big!" Leading the way, she slipped between the twiggy branches.

"We made a door," whispered Jackson. "A door-a-door-a-door-a-door!" he chanted softly, drumming the air.

"Shut up!" Tracey snapped. "Stop drumming! You want to wake the dead?" Jackson fell silent.

"Come *on!*" commanded Tracey. Tessa followed obediently. Pete came next, twisting sideways to get through the narrow gap. The caterpillar skin caught on twigs as Jackson, last of all, struggled through. It was a sleeping bag.

"No one could hear me drumming," he said to Tracey.

"The dead might," she said. Her matter-of-fact voice was more scary than a ghostly one. "They hear all! Right now they can hear us entering their kingdom. That's scientifically proven."

They were in the graveyard. There was an old grave beside them with a little wooden picket fence around it. Some of the pickets had broken away. The grave grinned a pointed grin, with a few teeth missing. Pete looked past it. Moonlight gleamed on the edges of stone after stone, stepping down the hillside in an irregular stair.

Off they went between the graves. There were flat, sealed graves with neat headstones, and untidy, sprawling ones where flowers and weeds had taken over. Some graves were small, narrow, and plain. Some were covered with slabs as big as tables. Chipped urns, fingers of marble, and gray angels with bowed heads rose up every now and then. Pete noticed one angel that had had both wings broken off. He felt sorry for it—it could never fly again.

Then Tracey stopped so suddenly that they all bumped into one another.

"This is a good place," she said.

"What for?" asked Pete, trying to sound slightly bored.

"For sleeping! That's the test. You have to sleep all night in the graveyard."

Pete suddenly switched on the torch and shone it on her face. Just as he had suspected: she was smiling slyly. "Look down there, not at me!" she cried. "There's grass between those two stones. It'll be comfortable there. I've brought a pillow, and Jackson's brought a sleeping bag for you."

"Mine!" said Jackson. "It's my sleeping bag, man!"

"You can keep it," Pete said. "It's not cold." He was surprised at how calm his voice sounded.

"No, go on!" said Tracey. "It gets really cold here after midnight, even on the hottest night. Cold and clammy."

Pete took the sleeping bag as if he didn't care one way or the other. *I could stay here for an hour or two and then sneak home and get back into bed,* he thought. Jackson saw him smiling as he wriggled the sleeping bag up around his shoulders.

"He might sneak back again," said Jackson.

"Jackson's a thought reader," Tracey said. "Musical people can read thoughts. Okay, Pete! You've got to swear an oath. That's part of the test. Say 'I, Peter Fortune . . .' "

"I, Peter Fortune . . ." said Pete wearily.

". . . promise . . ."

". . . promise . . ." said Pete, secretly crossing his fingers so that it would not be a real promise.

". . . not to go sneaking back to the house, and if I even *think* of sneaking back, may bony hands come out from the ground and grab my ankles and drag me down forever."

Pete echoed Tracey, crossing his fingers even more tightly. Everyone in the world, he reckoned, was frightened of bony fingers grabbing them and pulling them down.

Tessa said nothing. Pete thought she looked a little worried, a little ashamed of what the Good Fortunes Gang was doing to another Fortune cousin, but Tracey was the one who was making the rules.

"Okay," Tracey said. "This is the practical test. All you have to do is spend the night here. That's all. You only have to do it once."

"Have you done it?" asked Pete.

"We live here. We've spent hours and hours in the burying ground," Tracey said haughtily.

But suddenly Pete was sure that, though Tracey and Jackson might have spent hours in the grave-yard, neither of them had ever slept a night there. If he did it, it would be like knowing more words to the Fortune family songs than they did. It would prove that he was not only braver than they were, but more of a Fortune too. And they would have to admit it.

Tracey tugged at Jackson's arm.

"We're going to be watching you," she said to Pete. "No sneaking back!"

"I won't sneak back," snapped Pete.

Tessa turned. She still hadn't said a single word. Tracey and Jackson turned too. Off they went down the path between the stones, Jackson with a skip in his step as if plain walking just wasn't good enough for him. Dark Tessa disappeared into the shadows almost at once, but the fair hair of Tracey and Jackson shone in the faint moonlight. From a distance they looked like graveyard angels come down from their plinths, walking around in the dark. As the path dipped downhill, it seemed as if they were slowly sinking into the ground.

Pete sank down in turn, down on the grass between the two headstones, hobbled by the sleeping bag. *If something did come for me, I couldn't run,* he thought. He put the pillow under his head and lay on his back, waiting for morning and staring at the moon, alone in the graveyard between two tall stones.

CHAPTER
10

"In the graveyard," murmured Pete to himself.

"Lying in the graveyard on my own, own, own,
Listening for the rattle of a bone, bone, bone."

He drew his elbows into the sleeping bag, next to
his warm, living sides so that they would not touch
the cold, still stone.

"Now!" he said aloud, as if he were going to
arrange things efficiently. Moving his arms carefully, he switched on the flashlight. The first thing
he saw was a pair of gray feet. Above the feet were
the straight, gray folds of a long robe. A chipped,
gray face stared down on him. It was another stone
angel with short curls, and a broken nose that

made it look like a boxer. The wind blew. Did the curls move? No . . . it was simply his own trembling hand, shaking the flashlight slightly so that the light trembled too.

Pete shut his eyes and tried to trick himself into thinking he was really in bed. Of course even if he were asleep in bed, he might be dreaming. His nightmare about the false family was a dream of losing everything that kept him safe . . . everything he loved. But lying between the graves, he found, to his surprise, the nightmare had made him tough in some way. It was as if he had been practicing for this test, even though he didn't know he would ever be tested.

"I'm not scared, not really," he told himself. But why, then, did he have his eyes squeezed shut?

Pete opened his eyes. He looked straight up into the sky, through thousands of miles, millions upon millions of miles, of space. All that sky, all that night that seemed to be pressing down upon him, was not really there. He thought as far as he could into the darkness between the clouds, and then as far again. There was no end to whatever it was he was looking into. As he watched, the sky opened a dark lid of cloud and looked down on him with a white lopsided, mad, moony eye. Pete and the night stared at one another, but the night looked away first—closing its clouds across the moon. Pete shut his own eyes quickly. Looking up suddenly from between the tombstones, he had taken infinity by surprise. Now it made new, enormous, unending sense. He had seen the stars many times, but this time he felt they had altered him forever.

Something rustled in the grass. It wasn't the wind. It was coming closer and closer. Bony feet, perhaps, busily bustling toward him. Closer . . . closer . . . right beside him! Pete screwed up his eyes, tighter and tighter, but then he felt he had to know the worst. His eyes sprang wide open as if his eyelids were on powerful springs. At the same moment he switched on the flashlight. Something small and spiky scuttled away from the light. A hedgehog! There were no hedgehogs in Australia. This was the first time in his life he had ever seen one.

Pete was so interested that he forgot his fear. Sitting up, he tried to follow the hedgehog with the light. But it moved off quickly and, before he could get a proper look at it, vanished into the night, scrambling away on surprisingly long legs.

Seeing the hedgehog comforted Pete, though

he couldn't think why. It was like finding signs of life on an unknown planet. Lying back again, he thought spiky, hedgehog thoughts rather than bony, graveyard ones, and perhaps he did go to sleep quite accidentally. He couldn't quite remember, when he thought about it afterward. All he remembered was that he was staring into the sky again. The clouds had drifted by. The moon shone down.

The ground under the sleeping bag seemed to have grown lumpier and harder. He was warm enough, but the earth's bones were coming up through its skin of soil. Its ribs were grating against his. Pete sat up and turned on the flashlight again.

Far away, on the other side of the hedge and the Fortune family forest, he could hear voices singing. His parents and grandparents, his uncles and aunts, were singing old songs. Someone was playing a banjo. *That must be Dad.* Someone else was playing a violin. *And that must be Aunt Lorna. Everyone says she's a good fiddler.*

"I scream, you scream, we all scream for ice cream," Pete heard them sing. He longed to be in the light with the singing and the laughter. After all, he was the one who knew all the words.

The bones of the earth pressed up through the

sleeping bag. Once more Pete sat up and turned on the flashlight so that he could see how to work himself into a more comfortable position. He shone it on the stone on his right and lit up the inscription on the headstone. Out of the corner of one eye Pete made out sorrowful words: SADLY MISSED. Above that there was a name, partly in shadow, but still readable. Pete read it and froze. It was as if the stone were whispering to him.

PETER TWEED FORTUNE, AGED TEN. His own name! His own age! He was looking at his own gravestone! His traveling, family life, parents, Simon, Bombshell, and the cousins—they were nothing but dreams . . . the dreams of a ghost who thought he was still alive. And at that moment, as he stared in horror, he heard footsteps . . . no, he *felt* footsteps. He felt them tremble in the ground, felt them run through his hands and into his arms and shoulders, up his neck and into his head, where they blundered like moths against a lighted window. No hedgehog this time. Footsteps.

Pete turned his head away from the name on the tombstone and looked into the dark. A white blob was bouncing toward him, its edges fluttering in the graveyard wind.

CHAPTER 11

The white blob blobbed toward him. Pete fell flat on his back and lay there, wishing he were invisible. Little night breezes ran across his face.

Even if the ghost fell on him and he screamed, what good would it do? The Good Fortunes Gang would not come rushing to save him. The singing Fortunes would never hear him. A shriek rushed up through his throat, but he stopped it firmly with his teeth. Only a small, thin squeak got through to the outside world.

"Peter!" called an eerie voice. Nobody ever called him Peter. That was the name on the tomb.

Then another voice spoke.

"He'd never come here in a million years," it

said. "Just living next door to the graveyard frightens him."

That wasn't a ghost. That was Simon . . . Simon, whose blackness made him invisible in the night.

"Those *kids*!" exclaimed the first voice, sounding more ordinary this time. "Oh, I think I've torn my lace tights!"

Peter felt the scream behind his teeth dissolve. He opened his mouth, and all that came out was a little sigh. Then he sat up and switched on the flashlight. Someone yelled with fright, but it wasn't him. It was Simon.

"Peter!" said the first voice, and this time it didn't sound eerie or strange. "Wow! You nearly frightened the life out of us." It was Prue. Beside her, Simon clasped his hands to his black chest as if he were struggling to keep his heart inside him. Prue looked cool and easy.

"The pigs!" she cried. "I could turn them all into bacon!"

"How did you know I was here?" asked Pete.

"Lolly heard the others talking earlier, and then she heard you going out. She didn't exactly want to tell tales on the others. But she crept out and came and told me so that I could get you back into bed before your mother came home and found you missing."

"Just as well Mum didn't find your bed empty. She'd have been frantic," said Simon. "But I don't suppose you kids thought of that."

"You have to go through the test to join the gang," said Pete.

"No, you don't," said Prue scornfully. "None of them would ever spend a night in a graveyard, even a friendly one."

"Friendly!" exclaimed Pete softly, looking around. "A graveyard *friendly?*"

"Well, this one's friendly," said Prue. "There are a lot of Fortunes here! I used to play on their graves when I was little."

"Anyhow, I'm the only one that's allowed to give you nightmares," Simon said. "That's a brother's job, not a cousin's."

"That stone's got my name on it," Pete said, pointing.

"Far out!" said Simon. But Pete saw him shiver a little as he read the headstone.

"It's a great-uncle," said Prue. "Uncle Peter was named after that Peter, and you're named after Uncle Peter, so I suppose in a way it *is* your name. But it's not *you* that's buried there. That particular poor Peter drowned years ago. They found him in the sea and brought him home. So he's here, right next door to the rest of us."

She held out her hand to Pete.

"Come on! I'll take you around and introduce you, so you know this nonsinging part of the family. It'll be another sort of family reunion."

Pete crawled out of the sleeping bag, feeling like a butterfly stepping out of a cocoon. Prue gathered up the sleeping bag and handed it to Simon, who tossed it over his shoulder. She carried the pillow herself.

"You take charge of the light," Prue told Pete. He and Simon followed her past little mossy fences, and headstones laid down like scattered pages. Some of them were decorated with white stone flowers set under glass domes. Pete saw stone doves and clasped hands nestling among the flowers.

Prue stopped in front of a stone as big as a double bed.

"Great-grandpa and Great-grandma Fortune!" she cried. "I used to dance on this stone when I was little."

"Dance?" said Simon, a disapproving vampire.

"Well, if it were me, I'd like to feel great-grandchildren close by," Prue answered. "I'd say, 'Go on! Dance! Dance! Let my bones feel you dancing.' "

By now the moon was shining down so brightly that Pete switched off the flashlight to save the battery. They moved on with Prue pointing out family names on headstones, like chapter headings in a rambling story.

"Of course I've other relations here who aren't Fortunes," she said over her shoulder. "But tonight's Fortune night."

There were graves of old Fortunes and graves of young ones . . . even the graves of three babies that had not lived long enough to be given names. BABY FORTUNE, it said on each of their headstones.

Prue sounded so fond of the stones and the buried relations that it suddenly seemed to Pete that he, too, had known them for a long, long while. Through the trees they could faintly hear Fortune family songs being sung in their grandparents' house.

"When father papered the parlor, you couldn't
    see Pa for paste.
Dabbing it here! Dabbing it there! Paste and
    paper everywhere!

Mother got stuck to the ceiling, the kids got
  stuck to the floor.
You never saw a blooming family so stuck up
  before!"

"They're singing the old songs," said Prue.

"We know them," said Simon proudly. "Well,
Pete knows every one of them by heart."

The song stopped suddenly, but none of them
took any notice.

They had moved in a wide circle and were
standing by the gap in the hedge through which
Tracey, Jackson, Tessa, and Pete had entered the
graveyard. The old fenced grave with the missing
picket was still grinning at them, but by now its
grin was a friendly one.

There was a loud bump on the other side of the
hedge.

Pete turned to Prue. Simon drew a deep breath.
Prue merely put her finger across her lips and
stepped back into the shadows.

"He'll be scared, scared, scared," said a voice in
a whispered chant. "I'll bet he's quaking. I'll bet
he's shaking."

A figure with pale hair pushed itself through

the hedge. It was followed by another one, and then a third, darker figure.

"Not too close," Tracey said. "We'll stand in the shadows and moan."

"Oh, man!" said Jackson. "He'll be scared. Not just a little bit scared, but *big* scared, *enormous* scared, *infinity* scared."

He doesn't even know what infinity means, thought Pete in amazement, looking at Simon. *But I do . . . I looked right at it and it looked back at me. It's gone now, but I know it's there.*

Simon and Peter both looked at Prue. It seemed they could all understand each other without saying a word.

"He's going to be aghast," Jackson went on as he and Tracey moved by so close to Pete that he could have touched them. "A guest aghasted by a ghost. A guest a-ghosted by a ghost."

He was dancing a little, but Pete knew—knew for certain—that Jackson was the ghost ready to be a-ghosted by the guest.

"It's a bit mean," said Tessa. "I mean, he hasn't done anything to us."

"He's taken my bedroom," Tracey growled. "Ready? One! Two! Three!" She peered toward

the place where she thought Pete was still lying. "Moan!"

Slowly Prue lifted her arm. Simon and Pete watched it rise through shadows shot with moonlight.

Tracey and Jackson began a weird moaning . . . a terrible sound that would have horrified Pete if he had still been lying on his own between the two gravestones, being looked at by infinity.

Prue brought her arm down as if she were conducting a orchestra.

Simon cackled hideously, Pete howled. Together all three of them leaped out of the darkness onto Tracey, Tessa, and Jackson.

"Gotcha!" shouted Prue.

Three shrieks of terror rose up out of the old graveyard.

And at that moment, faintly but clearly, Pete heard someone far off in the darkness call his name.

CHAPTER
12

Jackson fell in a heap on the ground and lay there mumbling, "Man, oh man, oh man!" Even in his terror he twitched, as if he were dancing. Rather more slowly, Tessa collapsed beside him, both hands clasped across her face.

Tracey, panting, looked at Prue, Pete, and Simon.

"So you scared me! Big deal!" She did her best to sound ordinary, but her voice was high and trembling.

"You were being unkind to a *cousin*," said Prue, taking the flashlight from Pete and shining it straight into Tracey's face.

"We were just testing him," said Tracey.

"Suppose his mother had found he was miss-

ing?" asked Prue. "She'd have been worried frantic. And anyway, you kids shouldn't be wandering around in the dark."

"Back before you were married, you used to sneak out and go to parties," said Tracey rebelliously.

"Man, oh man! I'm dead!" sighed Jackson, still lying on the ground and writhing in time to his own words. "Dead, dead, and never been wed."

"Dead, dead, and out of bed!" Pete said so that other people could hear his rhymes as well. In the beam from the flashlight he saw Jackson's eyes snap open. He stared up at Pete as if this new cousin had spoken a secret password.

"It's because I used to be so silly that I know it *is* silly to sneak out at night," said Prue to Tracey. Tracey pulled a scornful face.

"Great!" she said. "You've turned into a grownup."

"That's right," Prue agreed. "I *am* grown-up. And you're just a kid. And you were being *cruel*."

"Not cruel!" cried Tracey. But for the first time she sounded ashamed. "It's just that he's a . . . well, he's only just come here and he's living in the old house and sleeping in my old room that I didn't want to leave, *and* he's been having a party in his honor."

Jackson scrambled to his feet.

"What a night!" he said. "What a night, what a night! What a terrible fright."

"My heart nearly stopped, but it didn't quite," finished Pete. Jackson turned and stared at Pete once more. Then, slowly, he began to grin. Tracey took no notice of them. She wheeled around on Tessa.

"Did you tell on us?" she asked.

"*I* saw you kids setting off," Prue replied, lying a little. "Come on, Trace. You were being mean to a new cousin."

"Pete!" called a faint, distant voice. Pete heard it distinctly. His ear was trained to hear his mother calling.

"Well, it's like that prodigal-son story," Tracey complained. "My dad stayed at home and helped the grandies, and he's never once had a party in his honor. It's not fair."

"Being mean to a cousin doesn't make it any fairer," said Prue severely.

"Come on, you kids! Where are you hiding?" shouted another voice—a man's voice. It was far off—on the other side of the house—but this time Prue, Simon, Jackson, Tracey, and Tessa heard it too.

"Oh, spattzz!" said Pete and Simon together.

"They know we've gone!" cried Jackson.

"They were singing just a moment ago," Tracey said, looking around as if uncles and aunts might suddenly appear out of the shadows.

"I expect your mothers came over to check up on you, and found you were gone," said Prue. She turned away, cupped her hands around her mouth, and shouted, "Over here! They're over here."

"Coo-ee!" called Pete.

"You sound Australian," said Jackson, looking pleased.

Somewhere someone heard them. They heard a voice call, "Findlay, they're on the other side of the house."

Tracey looked sideways at Pete. "We're up the creek now," she said, scowling. "My lot'll be really mad with me."

"Me too," Pete said. "But it was good to get out of bed and come down here. That's the sort of thing you can do when you've got a home, even at midnight."

As he said it, he felt for the first time that he

was at home. Tracey might have been trying to frighten him, but her test had worked in a way she hadn't expected. It had broken a spell. For one thing Pete knew he would never be afraid of the graveyard again. It seemed to him that he could feel his past family lying peacefully in the land behind him as the present family came storming toward him through the night. There would never, ever be any bony fingers reaching through the hedge to try to grab him as he went past. The angels looking over the hedge were smiling because they were pleased to see him.

Tracey was watching him. Pete could tell she was trying to work out if he was mad at her and what he was going to tell the grown-ups. In the flashlight beam he could see the beginning of a smile, but not an angelic one. It was too mischievous for any angel—a little bit ashamed and a little bit shy.

She opened her mouth to say something, but then they heard approaching voices. Footsteps thudded around the corner of the house. A stronger light swept across the house side of the hedge. Bits of it slipped through the leaves and fell in a scattered, jiggling jigsaw puzzle of brightness around them.

"I thought I heard someone screaming!" an aunt was saying.

"It was just us chickens cackling," called Prue. Turning, she struggled through the gap in the hedge. Tracey, Jackson, Tessa, Simon, and Pete followed her. On the other side of the hedge the light seemed as bright as a small sun. Pete couldn't see past it, but he recognized the voices. He turned off his own light. On the other side of the hedge were his uncles, aunts, grandparents, and parents. For the last time that night he looked over his shoulder and smiled at the dead Fortune family, then he climbed through to the live ones.

"It was just one of those midnight worraworras!" Tracey was saying. "Fortune kids always have a worraworra!"

"Worraworra worraworraworra" was what Tigger had said outside Pooh's house when he was a stranger in the forest. "Worraworra" was what Fortune children had cried to one another playing hide-and-seek in a darkened house. "Worraworra!" they would growl, crawling from room to room, making a scary party for themselves.

"We were crawling around in the dark trying to find each other," explained Pete, backing up

Tracey, and it suddenly seemed a brilliant descrip-
tion of what really had been going on.

"And you did find each other, even out here?"
asked an uncle. Pete recognized Uncle Peter's
voice.

"Well, I found a few people," said Simon.

"Me too," said Trace the Ace, and she smiled
sideways, slyly, at Pete.

"Oh, Pete," said his mother. "Why do you
frighten me like this? It was nearly as bad as the
time you tied that rope from the chimney to the
tree and tried to slide along it."

"Did you try to slide from the roof?" asked
Tracey.

"Don't growl at him, Maddy," said Pete's father. "It wouldn't have been a real family reunion
without a worraworra."

"Well, I'll forgive them this time," said Maddy.
"And I'm going inside to make a cup of tea. This is
a formal invitation for everyone to have one with
me . . . if I can find a few cups, that is."

There was a chorus of agreement from the
other Fortunes, and they all began to drift toward
the house that was now Pete's home.

"You're never, never to sneak out at night

again," he heard someone telling Tracey. Pete knew without turning around that it was Aunt Tiffany, and realized that he was beginning to know just who was who.

CHAPTER
13

A little later Pete sat in the shadows of the hall with all his cousins around him—except one, that is. Tracey seemed to have wandered off on her own.

Pete was sharing the bottom step of the stairs with Tessa. Lolly, who had been waiting for them when they all came trooping in, sat on the step above them. Pete's hands were clasped around a small enamel bowl of weak tea, enjoying its warmth.

None of the houses he had lived in had ever had such a big kitchen. The bottom step of the stairs was like a seat in a theater, and the kitchen, its door wide open, was like a lighted stage. Fortunes sat around the big table in the middle of the room, sometimes even on the table. Other Fortunes had settled themselves on packing cases, drinking tea from anything Maddy had been able to find. Maddy herself had her tea in a small jug, and Toby held a vase. There's something about drinking tea out of jugs and vases—because no one can remember just which packing case the cups are in—that stops people being too cautious with one another. What was going on in the kitchen was even more of a family reunion than the gathering on the lawn next door. Sitting on the bottom step of the stairs, Pete listened carefully, disentangling what the Fortune family were saying to one another. Only one person seemed to be worried about the happenings of the evening.

"But listen," Uncle Ivor was saying, "they all went wandering around in the dark when they were supposed to be in bed. Suppose there had been some sort of accident?" He had been given tea in a small pottery bowl, and as he talked, he looked down at it with a puzzled frown as if he wasn't quite sure how it had gotten into his hands.

"Oh, Ivor, don't be so stuffy," said Aunt Lorna. "We Fortune kids often used to get out of bed and have a worraworra in the bush."

"It's almost as if we had had a worraworra all

over again ourselves," Uncle Findlay was saying to Toby. "Remember that time when . . . ?"

"It was just dreadful when I looked into his room and saw he was missing," Maddy was telling Prue. "I thought he had run away. Trying to get back to Brisbane, perhaps."

"Brisbane! When he's got the chance of living in Fairfield?" said Prue, laughing. "No way! He'll never want to go back there again."

"Are you kidding?" said Maddy. "Queensland's full of New Zealanders trying to get away from the cold."

"I was sure they'd be in the bush somewhere," Grandma Fortune was saying to Aunt Marama. "I never once thought of the graveyard."

"I knew it would be something to do with Tracey," Aunt Tiffany exclaimed, interrupting Maddy and Prue. She was holding her baby, Angel, in her arms. Maddy was holding Bombshell, and Prue was holding Janey. The three babies looked solemnly at one another.

In the doorway, half in, half out of the kitchen, leaned Simon. Pete felt sorry for him. There were no cousins his own age to talk to, and he no longer had the fun of teasing Pete about ghosts and graveyards. Pete helped himself to a finger of toast and a

sliver of cheese from the plate at his feet. At least his mother had found the toaster. He noticed Tessa frowning down at his plate.

"We'll get biscuits later on today," he said.

"I like toast," said Tessa. "I was just looking for the best piece."

Jackson, who was sitting on the step behind them, leaned over and breathed toast crumbs into Pete's ear.

"Man, you scared the life out me," Jackson said. "My heart just stopped. Bang! Then it started off again, rapping away twice as fast. Wicked, man, just *wicked*!"

"But you were trying to scare *him*," said Lolly. "It's fair that he scared you back."

"Oh, yeah! I know," said Jackson. "But man, oh man! You let that scream off in my ear, and wow! Bang! I nearly died of fright."

"One moment frightened of a ghost, and now you're eating buttered toast," said Pete.

"Right on, man!" cried Jackson, laughing heartily.

Pete thought his mother looked much happier and easier than she had earlier that day. As for his father, he and Uncle Findlay and Uncle Peter were loudly criticizing one another.

"That's just like you!" "What absolute rubbish!" "How can you tell? *You've* never even been out of New Zealand." "Well, all I can say is, Australia's rotted your brain, mate." Their voices rose and fell, but they were laughing. They sounded much more like brothers than they had on the lawn next door.

Jackson lurched. Someone had come downstairs, pushing past him as if he were merely a branch in the way.

"It's funny," said Tracey's voice over Pete's head. "I've just been in my old room, but it doesn't feel like mine anymore. Without our things it doesn't look like home." She bent over the plate of toast and took two pieces. As she did this, she looked sideways at Pete and pulled an unexpectedly funny face. Pete could barely see her in the shadows, but he knew it was a sign of goodwill.

His old nightmare and the horror of all the familiar things deserting him flitted into his head, but it had no power to frighten him now. Tracey, Jackson, and Tessa hadn't actually said that they would let him join the Good Fortunes Gang, but he could feel that he was one of them now. He was a Fortune, sitting in the light of the kitchen with a family around him.

Suddenly the idea of having a big family took hold of him, and with the idea came an unexpected plan. Tomorrow he would begin making a family tree, and nobody would be left off. He would mark in his Australian relations, too, and all the people who had names other than Fortune. And when he was properly settled in as a member of the Good Fortunes Gang, he would make them allow Lolly to be a gang member too. He'd have to wait a while of course. He knew it was a mistake to throw one's weight around too soon. Still, he would do it.

As for the false sister, she would never be a menace or a mystery again. She was just his cousin Tracey. And though she had tried to frighten him, he had actually frightened her. He had turned her own trick back on her. From now on, this house would hold the family who lived in it safe during the hours of darkness. And the town would hold the house, and the stars and the sea would hold the town, and the universe would hold the stars and the sea. No one could be much more secure than that . . . being held by the universe. And everyone would be able to sleep peacefully.

Sitting there among his cousins, Pete knew that he had come home at last, while outside in

the moonlight on the quiet hillside other Fortunes
—old people and children, and some in between—
slept peacefully, too, still remembered, still part of
the family, and still safe at home.